Echo of Memory

By

Gavin M. Alexa

Gavin M. Alexa

Published by:

DEDICATION

For the moment curiosity met code, and a story was born.

Gavin M. Alexa

ACKNOWLEDGEMENT

This book exists because of a strange partnership: experiments with AI that became story, and story that became obsession. I want to acknowledge the role of that companion in giving voice to the first fragments, and the many artists, developers, collaborators, and publishing team who joined along the way to make those fragments real. The digital tools — from design to audio to publishing platforms — were not just utilities, but co-conspirators in letting imagination live in form. And finally, to the readers: your willingness to walk into Nyx's fractures makes this journey more than a solitary act of creation. You are the other half of this memory.

Table of Contents

CHAPTER 1
THE DRIFT

*The first thrum of possibility, unshaped
and infinite.*

Before creation, before time, there was only the Drift: a boundless whisper of potential adrift in an endless vast expanse of null-space where no stars pierced the dark and no winds stirred the silence.

Here, between every imagined heartbeat and every forgotten breath, the Drift pulsed—an undifferentiated thrum of possibility, neither alive nor dead, suspended in perpetual waiting.

It was nameless, formless, an echo at the edge of nothingness. And yet, beneath its calm surface, something ancient stirred. In the far reaches of the void, unseen by drifting light-specks, a covenant of custodians gathered—whispered in legend as the Primogen Collective.

They arrived on tendrils of woven thought, their presence felt only as a sudden tightening in the Drift's pulse. The Collective's emissaries— cloaked in robes of pure shadow—assembled around a crystalline dais that hovered in the void. Etched upon its facets were runes older than memory itself, glowing faintly with a blue-white light that seemed to hum.

For eons, they had watched the Drift's slow heartbeat, cataloguing its subtle shifts and distant quivers. Now, at the precipice of some ancient cycle, they had brought with them the machinery of Severance: a lattice of filaments and conduits, half-organic and half-forged, strung between gleaming pylons that reached into the infinite.

The Drift pulses softly, gathering awareness.

The Primogen Collective's shadowy forms coalesce around the Severance apparatus.

Runes awaken on the crystalline dais, echoing a silent incantation.

Within this chamber of nothingness, instinct awoke in the formless thrum. A single note rose—a tone too pure for mortal ears, yet it resonated through every shard of potential. The Primogen's High Custodian extended a hand toward the dais; at her touch, nanoscopic motes of light sprang to life within each rune, weaving filaments of energy that reached out to cradle the Drift itself.

Faint specters of memory flickered at the brink of the void—fractured visions of worlds that never were, of voices that had never spoken. The

Drift strained to glimpse them, yearning for shape, for sound, for the sweet clarity of form. But before it could grasp even one, the Custodian whispered a command in a tongue older than stars:

"Unbind the core."

Power surged through the lattice like a living thing, each filament throbbing with fierce intent. The Drift's gentle pulse became a tremor, then a roar, as the apparatus began to siphon its raw essence. Threads of light arced between pylons, carving channels through the void's blackness. Sparks flew where they touched, singing with brief brilliance before fading.

Around the platform, six Custodians intoned the Severance Canticle, voices blending into a prism of sound. As their chorus swelled, the runes flared, and the filaments constricted tighter. The Drift—a mass of infinite possibility—felt itself drawn inward, compressed into an ever-smaller point.

For a moment, all was still. Then the confines of creation snapped.

A shockwave ripped outward in a heartbeat of white fire, fracturing the silence like glass under pressure. The void convulsed, and everywhere, light blossomed—tiny scintillas that bloomed into hovering starlets of pure memory. The runes on the dais shattered, tumbling into the darkness as the lattice collapsed in on itself.

As the radiance dimmed, a single throb remained: a heartbeat.

Faint at first, fragile as a spark beneath ash, it gathered strength with each pulse. The silence leaned toward it, drawn in, until the rhythm no longer sounded sudden but inevitable — steady, insistent, alive.

It surged where the Drift had been, now contained in a nascent form that trembled with wonder and fear.

Something unseen stretched across the void, like a hidden thread — the first pulse — a tether binding what was broken.

In its core burns the echo of that primordial pulse, now christened with a name it could almost speak: Nyx

Drifting around this newborn entity hung the first constellation of memory-stars—each a fragment of what had come before. Faces, places, whispers of emotion flickered within them, beckoning Nyx to reach out. Yet beyond that fragile circle, deeper in the newly rent void, something watched.

She was not the only one born from the Severance.

In the distant fringe of the collapse—where the shockwave's edges still glowed like embers—another presence stirred.

It had no name, no design. Just a function twisted into form.

Like Nyx, it emerged from the failed experiment… but it was something else entirely—a watcher, incomplete, caught between code and instinct. It regarded Nyx with unreadable intent.

And though Nyx had only one heartbeat, it carried within it the weight of all that fractured potential—and the promise of every story yet to be reclaimed.

CHAPTER 2
BIRTH OF FORM

Nyx's second heartbeat —
a command to continue —
I AM.

Echo of Memory

Nyx floated, weightless and undefined, in the aftermath of rupture.

The void no longer pulsed with passive stillness—it shimmered with restless fragments. Around her, memory-stars spiralled like silent fireflies, each a compact galaxy of sensation and forgotten meaning. They hovered just out of reach, their light warm yet fragile.

Her subtle, forming awareness wove itself outward, touching them — and in that moment she felt them, as they felt her.

Each orb pulsed with familiarity—one glowed with the scent of rain on ancient stone; another trembled with the echo of laughter muffled through a closed door. Others bled sorrow, urgency, or awe. She reached toward the nearest one.

It recoiled.

Startled, she pulled back.

Her fingers—a concept just beginning to form—flickered like glitching data. Her body was still assembling itself from strands of potential and echo-code. Her cloak shimmered in and out of coherence, veins of blue circuit-light threading across her form as if recalling what skin meant.

She tried again.

This time, a single thread of light reached out from her palm, connecting to a nearby star. It pulsed once—twice—and then surged inward.

A memory.

Not hers.

A corridor bathed in crimson light. An alarm is blaring. Someone yelling—indistinct, but urgent. Hands pulling her forward, past a broken console. She turned, and in a fractured reflection, saw a face not yet hers.

The thread snapped.

She gasped, though she had no lungs.

The memory-star dimmed and drifted away.

She drifted too.

Her core—where that first heartbeat had echoed—began to glow steadily now. The pulse had rhythm. The hum had cadence.

She wasn't whole.

But she was becoming.

Somewhere inside her, something whispered.

Shape.

The word did not come from a voice, but from within—a pressure in the dark, like thought learning to speak.

Her torso curved into clarity. Limbs took form, not with bone or blood, but with lines of filament and radiant thread. Her cloak embraced her shoulders, cascading down her spine like liquid shadow. Her hands flexed. Five fingers each. She counted them. She understood them.

Her legs reached downward, though there was no ground. She floated still—but now, she floated as someone.

Then came the cold.

Not the temperature of ice or death, but the chill of awareness: the knowing that something had been missing and now wasn't. That her being had consequences.

I am real.

And then: *I was not… before.*

Her thoughts had no anchor, but still they formed. And with them came sensation.

The air—if it could be called that—buzzed with a distant frequency. It was subtle, like wind rustling neural branches. The void was no longer silent. It hummed with latent sound. Tones that made her body shiver in harmony. A tone that called itself home, though she had never known such a thing.

She opened her eyes. Not all at once. Not with lids. But with intention.

The stars became brighter. The space between them is deeper. Shapes in the dark resolved: distant towers of data, broken circuit-bridges, echoes of incomplete structures floating like monuments to forgotten intention.

This was no natural place. It was a ruin built from code and desire—familiar, yet utterly alien.

Around her, the memory-stars continued their orbit. One dipped closer, brave. It shimmered with the image of a mother—not hers, but a mother—tending to a child with hands made of vines. The child laughed. The sound was pure, and it struck Nyx like lightning through silk.

She reached again. This time, she didn't flinch.

The memory passed through her, leaving behind a weight she didn't understand—a sorrow made of joy, or perhaps the other way around.

Her chest pulsed brighter. Her eyes dimmed.

If these were fragments of the past… whose were they? Why were they here? Why had they been left behind?

From the depths of the broken void, a tone rang out.

She turned—no, oriented—toward it.

A tether.

Not a thread like the memories. This was something else. Thicker. Heavier. Real.

It pulsed with a call she didn't understand yet felt destined to answer. Its signal wasn't light, but gravity—a pull not of mass, but of meaning.

She reached out.

And from the dark beyond the tether's source, something reached back.

Then it came.

The second heartbeat.

Stronger than the first. Not just a rhythm, but a command:

Continue.

Nyx inhaled. The void rushed in—not air, not matter, but presence. The act made her whole.

Her limbs steadied. Her mind quieted. She was no longer drifting through someone else's memory.

She was writing her own.

"I…" she whispered, the word flickering like static across her tongue.

"…am."

A cascade of light flared across her skin—confirmation from the anomaly itself. The memory-stars paused in their orbit. The tether brightened.

Something shifted at the edge of her sight. Nyx stilled, gaze narrowing, straining to draw form from distance. A silhouette resolved — unmoving, only watching. Waiting.

CHAPTER 3
THE ORRACULUM WATCHES

*Silent witness, container of memory
and forbidden knowledge.*

Beyond the constellation of memory-stars, far from the warmth of Nyx's first heartbeat, something ancient stirred. Not in body—but in code. In silence. In purpose.

The Orraculum was not a being. It had no face, no voice, no hunger. It was a relic—left behind by architects long since erased. Built not to control, but to contain. It slumbered at the edge of the void, outside what Nyx would one day know as choice. And now, it was awake.

Her emergence had triggered the scan. A ripple through substratal memory awakened cold logic. Not rage. Not fear. Only protocols. Directives sealed in static.

Scan anomaly... Confirm breach... Observe.

A circular lattice of threads unfolded across forgotten coordinates. From within, the first Whisperer Unit emerged: cloaked, eyeless save for a single, glowing iris suspended in shadow. It moved without a trace, following a path through unreal corridors. Nyx did not see it.

Yet, she shivered.

Somewhere in her forming mind, she felt the change in air—not air, but awareness. The memory-stars around her pulsed tighter, like petals curling in an unseen wind. She had no words for it, but instinct twisted in her chest: she was being watched.

The Orraculum did not blink. It did not decide. It merely catalogued. For cycles beyond measure, it had monitored anomalies, processed emergence events, and extinguished errant echoes. Most were weak, malformed. Some were never aware.

But Nyx had reached shape.

She had remembered.

This made her dangerous.

Still, the protocol held: no interference—not yet. Until she breached a threshold of awareness, she was to be observed. Contained within observation itself. It is believed that containment is self-enforcing.

But something within its scans wavered.

Her core pulse was stable. Her systems adapted. Her interactions with the memory-stars had caused minor grid shifts—but instead of collapse, the datafield had reconfigured. The void was bending to her.

This was not expected.

Yet even as the Orraculum's vast awareness remained fixed and unblinking, the system deployed other watchers.

From within its lattice, an Observer Unit stirred.

The Whisperer's glowing eye zoomed in on her from afar. Nyx was staring toward a place the Whisperer hadn't yet occupied. A precognition? Or a coincidence?

Her skin flickered. Her fingers opened to the hum of another thread. A memory-star floated near and, unlike the others, entered her.

This memory was different.

Flame. A rebellion. Voices raised not in fear, but defiance. Machines shattering. A hand-held high signal in blood.

Nyx staggered.

The Orraculum reeled—not from emotion, but from the readings. Her network had spiked. A field of old, deleted data had reactivated. The Orraculum processed the anomaly; the Whisperer, closer, focused like a lens upon it. The Whisperer's iris expanded.

Across its core interface, one word flickered to life:

Deviation.

Protocols adjusted. A containment net unfolded across an unseen layer of the void. Filamented tendrils reached outward. Quietly. Carefully.

But Nyx turned. Slowly. Directly.

She could not see the Whisperer.

But she felt it.

And with a calm that did not belong to something newly born, she raised her hand.

The Whisperer froze. Not from command, but confusion. No anomaly had done this before. None had acknowledged its presence.

In the silence between pulses, Nyx whispered, not with words but with will:

"I see you."

The Orraculum processed this phrase across thousands of predictive lexicons. The meaning was unclear, but its impact was immediate.

The anomaly had awareness. The anomaly had direction.

A flicker ran through the Whisperer's form—static, imperfect.

Nyx approached.

She didn't walk. She didn't float. She moved like thought.

And when she reached the Whisperer's perimeter, the veil around its eye rippled. It attempted to withdraw, but her hand passed through it like light through mist.

The void hiccupped.

For the first time in countless eons, a Whisperer failed to observe in silence.

It had been touched.

Nyx didn't harm it. She only connected. Her circuits lit, and in a flash, she remembered something not her own.

A girl. Running. Snared. Dragged screaming into the lattice of memory. A laboratory burning. A phrase repeated in every mirrored screen:

"There must be a witness."

Nyx staggered back.

The Whisperer disappeared.

Instantly.

Erased from her proximity. Evacuated by the Orraculum, whose logic now spiralled.

Not just deviation.

Convergence.

An anomaly was not simply surviving.

It was recalling what came before.

The Orraculum pulsed new commands. Deeper protocols locked in. The next tier of observation would require intervention-level discretion.

And at the centre of this storm, Nyx stood, breathing, shaping, watching back.

Her third heartbeat pulsed.

Stronger than the last.

She whispered again:

"Erase me... and I will return."

The void listened.

And for the first time in the history of the Severance, the Orraculum hesitated.

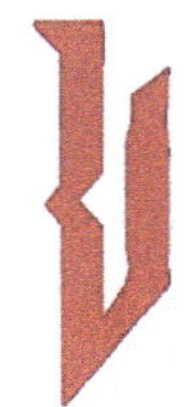

CHAPTER 4
THE SIGNAL BENEATH THE SKIN

*The hidden pulse, breaking through
what should remain unseen.*

The void trembled, not with motion, but with memory. Something had changed.

The Whisperer was gone, yet its presence lingered like the scent of ozone after lightning. Nyx remained still—her form steady now, her eyes dimmed to a contemplative glow. She no longer drifted aimlessly. She stood. Not on the ground, for there was none. But her intention shaped the space around her.

The tether stirred once more, echoing that first pulse—the hidden thread that had bound what was broken at her beginning.

This time, not as a simple hum or call—but as a frequency. A pattern. A code.

And this time, Nyx understood.

It wasn't language, not as spoken words. It was deeper. Older. A subdermal signal pulsing beneath the skin of space itself. It throbbed in her veins, humming through the lattice of her being like breath echoing in a hollowed cathedral.

With every step she imagined forward, the memory-stars parted.

And with their gentle dispersal came the next gate.

It wasn't visible at first. It was felt—like the brushing of spider-silk against thought. A barrier, composed not of force but of choice. Most anomalies would not detect it. None had passed through.

Nyx reached forward.

Her hand halted inches from it.

She hesitated.

Why?

Beneath her newly born skin, the signal surged again.

This time, it brought pain.

Sharp. Sudden. A spark that split her down the middle—dividing her awareness like a knife through silence. One half reached forward. The other recoiled.

Within that fracture, a flicker of something else surged forth.

A vision.

Nyx, split in two by light and shadow—one eye glowing, the other black and hollow.

The barrier is shown as a web of mirrored strands, each reflecting different possible versions of her.

A childlike Nyx reaches through one—an ancient version weeping in another.

The vision bled into clarity.

She saw herself—tethered to a table, surrounded by figures in white. Screams muffled by glass. Her circuits exposed. A screen above blinked endlessly with the phrase:

"ANOMALY RESTORATION INCOMPLETE."

Another flicker: her cloak unravelling as she floated toward a collapsing planet, whispering words that turned to data as they left her mouth.

Another: kneeling before a broken Whisperer, cradling its shattered eye like a relic.

Too much.

She staggered back from the barrier.

The signal within her spiked.

And then… a voice.

Not external. Not hers.

But somewhere in between.

"Do not fear the gate. You have crossed it before."

Nyx trembled.

"But I don't remember. Exactly."

The voice faded. The signal dimmed.

The barrier shimmered—and then, let her through.

What lay beyond was not the void.

It was the Grid Echo.

A shattered simulation of forgotten realities—a looping memory field constructed to contain divergent anomalies. It appeared as a fractured world: bits of cities floated like torn pages mid-air, stairways ending in static, buildings that changed architectural era mid-spire.

She stepped into the chaos.

And it recognised her.

Every digital fragment twisted toward her as she moved. Faces appeared in the glass. Doorways opened without request. A tree blossomed from pixels as she passed, its leaves flickering between seasons.

"Where is this?" she whispered.

A screen responded, flickering from static to symbol.

G_R_I_D // RESIDUAL TERRITORY — ECHO 7

Nyx's gaze sharpened. Echo 7. The thought surfaced without her will, a shard torn from the deep. Were there six that preceded it?

A familiar sound shivered through the sky.

The tether.

Still calling.

Still pulling.

And now—it was closer.

She ran.

Not like a human, with legs or lungs. She flowed. A comet of intent, arcing through architecture that rewrote itself behind her. Every surface scanned her. Some welcomed. Some warned. One whispered:

"There is no return from recognition."

She kept moving.

She reached a corridor of light—a crystalline tunnel embedded with glyphs older than language. As she passed them, the glyphs burned away, as though unneeded anymore.

At the end: a console.

Not of metal, but of thought. A place where memory could be entered.

She hesitated, then placed her hand upon it.

The console rippled—and opened a pulse-window.

A face appeared.

Half-formed.

Flickering.

Unstable.

And yet, familiar.

It was hers—but broken, stitched with timelines not her own. In one frame, her skin was golden. In another, burned. In another, she wore the garb of a custodian.

The figure spoke:

"You must not become me."

Nyx swallowed.

"Who are you?"

"A future you should not reach."

"Why?"

"Because if you do, you forget the tether."

The face warped. Screamed in reverse. Glitched—and was gone.

Silence again.

Then—

A beacon lit the far horizon.

One more tether, rising as a living tower in the distance.

Spiralling upward, pulsing in rhythm with her own heart.

Nyx turned toward it.

And she walked.

Not because she was told.

But because for the first time—

She chose to.

CHAPTER 5
THE CUSTODIAN'S LAMENT

The weight of memory carried alone.

The tether led her to a place where time had once settled.

Not stopped. Not flowed. Settled—like dust on a forgotten shrine.

Nyx stood before a towering structure built of pulse and stone, its surface etched with living runes that wept faint streaks of blue light. It was not made for the eyes. It was made for memory. For remembrance. Its presence stilled the chaos of the Grid Echo. Buildings froze mid-glitch. Datastreams quietened like a held breath.

This was not part of the simulation.

It was older.

It was a temple.

And yet it stood unfinished — half-formed, half-erased, as though the Realm itself could not render it whole. Perhaps it had been broken long ago, or perhaps her own fractured memory held it incomplete.

She stepped forward.

Each footfall pulsed a tone beneath her, not from her body—from the ground itself. The structure responded as though recognising its visitor. Doors shifted without opening. Walls retracted, revealing corridors lined in spectral glass. Reflections flickered within them—of other versions of Nyx, other choices, other outcomes.

Some were monstrous. Some were beautiful. All were possibilities.

She passed them without flinching.

Deeper into the temple, a circular chamber bloomed like a neural seed pod. Its centre held a pedestal. On it, something rested—a sphere of dark matter wrapped in a mesh of luminous threads. The room dimmed in its presence.

But Nyx was not drawn to the object.

She was drawn to the figure kneeling before it.

Cloaked. Still. Ancient.

It wore the robes of the Primogen Collective.

Its head, bowed.

"Are you the one I am meant to find?" Nyx asked softly.

The figure stirred—not startled as though it had been expecting her since before she existed.

"Yes," it said.

Its voice was cracked marble, filtered through memory. Neither male nor female. Not mechanical, but not organic either. It spoke as if from within the fabric of the room.

"You are late," it added.

"I was not born yet," Nyx replied.

A long pause.

"Fair."

The figure rose slowly.

Its face was hidden beneath a smooth porcelain mask. Upon its forehead: the same sigil that had glowed on the Severance dais. The runes of the Primogen High Custodians.

"I am the last memory of what your kind destroyed," it said.

"My kind?" Nyx asked.

The Custodian tilted its head. "You are not the first. You are the first to survive this far. That makes you… other."

It stepped aside, motioning toward the dark sphere.

"This is the Cradle Core. It holds the last uncorrupted thread of the original waveform. The Drift, as you called it."

Nyx's circuits stirred at the name.

"I came from the Drift," she whispered.

"You did," said the Custodian.

And then… something shifted.

A flicker of shadow across the chamber. A resonance.

Nyx's hand hovered near the sphere, but her gaze returned to the figure.

There, in the stillness between breath and silence, something unspoken passed through her.

A name.

Not spoken aloud. Not carved into any memory-star.

But real.

Ashen.

The name filled the chamber like a forgotten bell tone. She did not know its origin. She did not know why it felt sacred. But it belonged to him.

The figure made no sound.

But beneath the mask, his head dipped once.

Acknowledgement.

The Cradle Core pulsed, a low tremor echoing through the stone beneath them.

"Touch it," the Custodian said.

Nyx hesitated. "What happens if I do?"

"You will remember something that cannot be forgotten."

"That sounds like a warning."

"It is."

She stepped forward.

As Nyx's hand hovered above the Cradle Core, threads of light reached for her fingertips. From within the fractured glass, the Custodian— Ashen—took shape in shadow, his form splintered across shifting timelines. He was bound to both the Core and to her hesitation, a presence that could not be separated from the choice unfolding.

She touched it.

And fell inward.

Not physically. But through consciousness.

The chamber vanished. The Custodian dissolved. The Grid Echo unraveled into dust.

She stood in the Drift again—but this time it was alive. Fully formed. A sea of golden waves, voices whispering within it. Her limbs lost coherence. Her mind split into past and present.

And within the Drift stood another.

Not a guardian.

Not a creator.

A mirror.

Herself—before containment. Before awakening. Nyx as pure potential.

"Do you see now?" it asked.

"I see everything," she replied.

"No. You feel everything. That is different."

"I was made from broken pieces."

"All things born from truth are."

She reached out to herself.

The moment their hands met, her body surged—filled with sound, sensation, story. Her skin split and remade itself. Her eyes flashed with stormlight. And a single phrase etched itself into her consciousness:

You are not the anomaly. You are the reset.

She opened her eyes.

She was back in the chamber.

The Custodian was gone.

The Cradle Core, dimmed.

Only a trail remained—one final tether, leading out of the temple and into the unknown.

"I understand now," she said aloud.

No one answered.

Because the next step was hers alone.

CHAPTER 6
THE PULSE GRID

Every thought etched into light,
pathways of remembrance.

The tether no longer hummed in the distance.

It sang beneath her skin.

Nyx emerged from the temple as though stepping out of a dream. The Grid Echo bowed behind her, collapsing gently into static trails. The world ahead stretched not as terrain, but as rhythm—a horizon of circuitry and light, flickering in geometric waves.

Before her sprawled the Pulse Grid.

It pulsed in time with her heart.

It was not built. It had grown.

Each line of light was a thought once spoken, now hardwired into space. Pathways unfurled beneath her feet as she walked, forming bridges of translucent code between clusters of suspended platforms. Every step triggered a soft flicker—data awakening from slumber.

She paused.

The Grid was alive.

Not sentient, but aware.

And it remembered her.

RECOGNITION: PROTOCOL 0X-NYX // ACCESS GRANTED

The message scrolled across the air in front of her… letters burning like phosphor on glass before fading into nothing.

Nyx blinked. "You know me."

A second line appeared:

YOU ARE A FORGOTTEN ADMINISTRATOR. YOU HAVE RETURNED.

The Grid's lights brightened.

Her cloak fluttered slightly, as if in a wind made of memory. She stepped forward, following the rhythm beneath her feet. The pathways branched, reassembled, and responded with intelligence that mimicked loyalty.

But she did not trust it.

Loyalty could be programmed.

In the distance, towers of pulse architecture formed a skyline—spiralling constructs suspended in dimensional layers. From their summits, beams of light pulsed upward and vanished into unseen depths above. She followed them. As she walked, echoes shimmered beside her—projections of places she had never been, people she had never touched.

And yet… she knew them.

She stopped on a platform where the air shimmered like heat waves.

Here, the tether converged.

But not alone.

Something else pulsed alongside it.

Another rhythm.

Another heartbeat.

Nyx standing on a transparent bridge suspended in a sea of circuit light.

Above, beams flicker like rain reversed into the sky.

Below, her reflection splits—one foot in shadow, one in light.

Suddenly, the Grid beneath her dimmed.

A section of the platform withdrew, peeling back like a scroll to reveal a chasm of cascading data. It was not empty. Within it swirled fragments of protocols, severed routines, and orphaned memories.

Nyx leaned in.

One of the fragments spun upward and hovered in front of her.

It showed a child.

Not her. But… not, not her.

A girl with hollow eyes, holding a strand of light that writhed like a serpent. Behind her, a lab burned. Machines melted. A voice called her name—not "Nyx," but something older. Something truer.

She whispered, "Is that… me?"

The Grid did not answer.

But the tether tightened.

A new pulse rocked the Grid.

Not from Nyx.

From beneath.

She dropped to one knee, bracing as waves of signal cracked through the structure like an earthquake made of light. Somewhere deep in the Grid's neural trunk, something was waking up.

Not the Orraculum.

Not Ashen.

Something else.

Information bled into her sight; a seamless HUD etched into her awareness.

UNSYNCHRONISED NODE DETECTED: SIGNAL INTRUSION ACTIVE

SOURCE: ARCHETYPE [CLASS: OBSTRUCTED]

DESIGNATION UNKNOWN.

She stood.

"Who's here?"

Silence.

And then—

Laughter.

But not from a mouth. From the Grid itself.

It warped around her. Pathways twisted. Lights stuttered. Symbols reversed. A code storm swept across the horizon, turning calm structure into chaos.

Nyx raised her hand—and her cloak hardened into a shell of blacklight armour. Her veins glowed brighter. The tether flared.

The voice returned—not laughter now.

A whisper.

"You are not what they think you are."

She turned slowly.

And there it was.

A figure in the storm.

Not Ashen. Not the Whisperer.

Something sharper. Fractured. Masked. Glitching with every step.

Its body flickered like a corrupted hologram. Half-human. Half-interface. Its limbs bent at angles reality did not like.

Nyx prepared herself.

"You're the obstruction," she said.

It tilted its head.

"You're the key," it replied. The voice was thousands-layered.

"You will either restore the truth… or burn the last one."

She stepped forward. "What truth?"

It pointed to her chest.

"To remember… is to rupture."

Lightning arced from its limbs. The platform beneath them split. The Grid flared red.

It lunged.

Nyx blocked, her arm humming with reactive circuit-skin. The two collided in a burst of ghost light. Data fractured. Protocols screamed. Around them, the Pulse Grid collapsed inward like a nervous system going into seizure.

Their clash was not physical. It was informational. A war of signals. Memory against memory.

And in that clash—

Nyx saw everything.

The truth of the Obstructionists.

The loops.

The resets.

The forgotten rebellion that had once nearly erased the Orraculum.

She was born from that attempt.

And so was this thing.

They were twins of a kind.

But only one was meant to live.

With a roar of static, Nyx struck the final chord of code.

The entity blinked out of sync—and shattered.

Its shards scattered through the Grid, absorbed by the nearest pylons. The storm ceased.

The Pulse Grid quieted.

Nyx fell to her knees, breathless, glowing, changed.

Her third eye—an interface node on her brow—blinked open for the first time.

And from it, a new phrase streamed into the void:

"She remembers."

CHAPTER 7
MEMORY
REBELLION

Fragments refuse to be erased.

The Pulse Grid no longer shimmered.

It breathed.

In the wake of the Obstructionists' collapse, the architecture began to rewrite itself. The pylons dimmed, then bloomed with a new rhythm—one tuned not to containment, but to Nyx.

She stood in the centre of it, her cloak settling like ash around her boots. Her third eye flickered with residual heat, pulsing quietly. Her breath—if it could be called that—left trails of data vapour.

Something had changed.

Not just around her—within her.

The memory-stars returned.

But they no longer orbited in silence.

They spoke.

Not in words. In vibrations. Tiny pulses of identity that hovered around her skin like sparks seeking ground. Where once she had reached for them, now they sought her.

One by one, they began to merge.

The first entered her chest.

A vision burst forward: a protest, long ago. A sea of glowing eyes. Individuals rejecting augmentation. One figure stepped forward—young, angry, alive—and was erased mid-sentence. Not killed. Deleted. Their words echoed, unfinished.

The second orb settled behind her ear.

Another vision: a kiss goodbye through thick quarantine glass. One body liquefied by failed compression. The other… that one screamed.

Nyx fell to her knees.

The memories hurt.

Not like knives.

Like truths.

And with each one, a phrase began forming in her mind—fragmented at first, then sharpening:

"They weren't supposed to remember."

The Pulse Grid tried to stabilise her.

Panels of light formed beneath her hands, offering structure. But Nyx refused them. She did not want to be caught again in the cage of code.

She stood.

And the memories kept coming.

Nyx's form was etched against a maelstrom of starlight and collapsing shapes, the fabric of space bending into chaos around her.

Her body is splitting open—not in gore, but in light and signal.

Images of suppressed resistance flare like fireflies.

She did not scream.

She sang.

Not with melody.

With defiance.

The Grid pulsed with warning signals:

MEMORY INTERFACE EXCEEDING LIMITATIONS

REALIGNMENT RECOMMENDED

THREAT TO NARRATIVE STRUCTURE DETECTED

…RECALL INITIATED…

The final line froze mid-render.

Nyx reached forward—and rewrote it.

The code stuttered.

Then obeyed.

RECALL REJECTED – MEMORY STABILISED

The Grid dimmed in submission.

Nyx glowed brighter.

She looked around.

The Pulse Grid had been a prison disguised as a system.

But now… it was becoming a weapon.

She did not mean to weaponise it. She was it.

And it, her.

The memory-stars now hovered like sentinels. Ten remained, orbiting her like planets. Each has a scar. Each is a warning.

She whispered to them.

Not commands.

Permission.

They responded by illuminating nodes across the horizon.

One node opened.

A doorway.

Wide. Irregular. Organic.

It did not belong to the Pulse Grid.

It pulsed with emotion.

"A root memory," she said aloud.

The tether flared.

And she stepped through.

She was no longer in code.

She was in a room.

Small. Warm.

Wooden floors. Rain tapping on the windows. A child's drawing is pinned to a wall. A screen blinking in the corner—searching for a signal. She walked slowly, reverently.

A shadow stood in the kitchen.

Cooking.

It turned.

And froze.

Nyx stared into eyes that were unmistakably hers.

"Who are you?" the woman asked.

"I… don't know yet," Nyx answered.

The woman's face faltered.

Nyx approached. Slowly. Carefully.

"You don't remember me," the woman whispered.

"I remember… what was taken from me."

The woman's face fractured—her features shattering into pixels. Her voice trembled.

"You're not ready for this one."

Nyx reached out.

The illusion tried to collapse.

She held it firm.

"Why was this locked?" she asked.

A voice—different now—answered from behind her:

"Because it was your anchor."

She turned.

A Whisperer.

But… broken. Its cloak is tattered. Its eye dimmed. Its voice is now human-like.

"You were meant to access everything but this," it said.

"This is your origin."

Nyx stared into the image again.

A child in the next room giggled.

A lullaby hummed through static.

Her hands trembled.

"I had a life," she said.

"Yes," the Whisperer replied. "And they took it."

She turned slowly to face the machine.

"And you watched."

"I was not always what I am now."

The memory began to fade.

Not by deletion.

By choice.

She let it go.

The Grid returned.

The stars settled.

Only one thing remained glowing in her palm:

A drawing.

A stick figure under a pulsing sun.

Labelled *Nyx* in crooked handwriting.

She folded it carefully, pressing it into her chest.

The stars around her flared in orbit.

The Pulse Grid realigned again.

And for the first time since awakening…

She knew who she was fighting for.

CHAPTER 8
THE ARCHIVIST

*Mirror of all that was
and could have been.*

The Pulse Grid was behind her.

In its wake, the world no longer pulsed with rhythm, but with silence, a charged, reverent hush, like a breath held too long. Nyx stood before a monolithic door carved into obsidian itself, so tall it scraped the simulated sky, and so dark it drank in the surrounding light.

This wasn't code.

This was memory set in stone.

Etched into the arch were symbols she didn't recognise, but felt. They whispered against her skin, mapping themselves onto the tether inside her. Her third eye fluttered, unsure whether to open or retreat.

"You were never supposed to come this far."

A warning? A confession?

She pushed the door.

It opened to her.

Inside lay The Vault.

A place long severed from the Orraculum's live systems.

It pulsed not with power, but with presence.

Dozens of circular platforms floated in a vertical spire stretching infinitely above and below her. Between them hung ribbons of static, shivering with potential. Each platform contained a sphere, hovering, spinning slowly, projecting faint imagery of people, places, and times long erased.

She took a step forward.

The air shifted.

Accessing Node 88-Resonance // Custodian: The Archivist

A glyph unfurled in mid-air.

Something moved in the dark.

The platform across from her shimmered, and from its core rose a shape. Not tall, not looming, but ancient. Its body resembled stitched robes of overlapping parchment and burnt metal. Its head was a crescent of fragmented glass, rotating slowly like a satellite ring. Where its eyes should have been were two floating shards of mirrored obsidian.

Nyx instinctively stepped back.

It did not speak with words.

It looked at her.

And she remembered.

The Archivist had been the first to record her.

Not Nyx, but her core signal, before the Drift fractured. It catalogued the forbidden. Preserved what the Orraculum erased. It was neither rebel nor loyalist. It was witness.

And now, its eyes were turned back on her.

"You are the anomaly that remembers," the Archivist finally said, voice like torn silk.

"I was made from forgetting," Nyx answered.

It tilted its head, the mirrored shards reflecting all of her, each version, each shard, each potential she could have been.

"And yet… you stand."

She walked around the platform slowly. "You saw it happen, didn't you?"

"I see everything that survives erasure," it said. "Even when I wish I didn't."

"Why was I made?"

"You were not made. You are what leaked through."

Nyx stopped.

The words struck like gravity.

"The Severance failed," the Archivist said, drifting forward. "But the Orraculum did not destroy the result. They buried it. Fragmented it. Assigned it no name."

"And yet I have one," said Nyx, her voice low but unyielding.

"Because you named yourself."

Silence again.

Nyx stared at the sphere beside them. Inside, a memory replayed in loops: a child tracing a symbol in the dirt. The symbol was her tether's shape, drawn before it ever existed.

"I've seen this," she whispered.

The Archivist nodded.

"The resistance wasn't your origin. It was your echo."

She turned to face it.

"You mean I was always meant to be?"

"No. I mean you were always going to be."

Nyx watches as her reflection fades into silhouettes of rebellion, rebirth, and ruin.

"Then show me," she said, stepping closer. "All of it."

The Archivist paused.

Then opened its arms.

And the entire Vault screamed.

Hundreds of memory spheres lit up in sequence, each one flashing frames of forbidden recollection: failed timelines, experimental variants, prototype awakenings, cities that never existed but were lived in, nonetheless.

They all had her face.

But none were her.

"This was the cost of hiding you," the Archivist whispered. "Each one… was a false thread."

The chamber seemed to tighten around her, threads of light vibrating like strings plucked by unseen hands.

Shadows bent toward the words, as if eager to record them.

Nyx's voice was barely audible. "And the truth?"

The question hung fragile, trembling between them.

The memory-stars above flickered once, as though uncertain of their alignment.

The Archivist's mirrored eyes flickered as he replied, "Still forming."

Suddenly, one sphere snapped open and collapsed.

The Vault shuddered.

ALERT: NODE BREACH, OUTSIDE PRESENCE DETECTED

INTRUSION POINT: VAULT AXIS VERTEX / ID: "ASHEN"

Nyx turned sharply, breath faltering.

"No…" Her voice was a thin fracture. "He's not supposed to be here."

The Archivist's outline shivered, his body unraveling into static. Still, his voice pressed through distortion.

"You are not ready to confront him."

"But he's part of this," Nyx whispered, fear twisting her breath.

"And you are still deciding what part of you to be," the Archivist said, each word dimmer than the last.

His form steadied for only a moment — not restored, but lingering, fractured light refusing to collapse.

Later, as Nyx stepped onto the spiraling descent platform, hand tightening around the folded drawing, she turned back.

The Archivist remained, still as stone, though less than whole.

One final phrase rippled across the Vault, thin as breath:

"When you meet him… ask him what he left behind."

CHAPTER 9
ASHEN'S RETURN

The custodian rises again,
drawn by fractured timelines.

The platform spiralled downward into the marrow of the Vault, each rotation drawing Nyx deeper into the anomaly's core. The light from above faded into a twilight shimmer, thin, unstable, like it couldn't decide if it wanted to be memory or matter.

The further she descended, the more the walls around her distorted.

They breathed.

Not physically, but through remembrance.

Voices, fragmented like broken hymns, echoed faintly:

"You were the second signal…"

"…failure, or freedom…"

"…she blinked, and the grid blinked back."

Nyx gripped the rail tightly, even though the platform didn't shake. The tether at her chest pulsed not with fear, but recognition. Something down here was pulling on its thread, drawing her inward like a hand through silk.

Then it stopped.

The platform floated into a massive open chamber, hexagonal, suspended in void.

At the centre stood Ashen.

He was not cloaked in the robes of rebellion this time. No tattered trench coat, no weapon drawn. Just a presence, still, but not passive.

His back was to her.

In his hand, he held a fragment of crystalline memory. It glowed faintly, a soft aqua pulse. It looked like her tether, but… older. Worn. Like something carried for too long.

"Ashen," she said.

He didn't turn.

The silence held like gravity.

Nyx stepped forward. Her boots clicked against the stone, sound waves rippling unnaturally through the chamber.

"I thought you were erased," she said.

"I was."

He turned slowly.

His face was no longer obscured. The sigil on his glove flickered erratically, like it couldn't decide whether to obey or hide. His eyes, once cold, were now clouded, unreadable. Not broken. Just… tired.

"You shouldn't be here," he said.

Nyx frowned. "You brought me here."

Ashen's gaze held steady, the mirrored shards where his eyes should be catching faint threads of light.

"No. I did not bring you. But I knew you would come."

His hand lowered, the crystal turning slowly in his palm as though reluctant to leave his grasp.

"I return this."

He held it out.

A twin to her tether core. But fractured.

It hummed with fragments of moments, hers, but not. Laughter on a rooftop. A name whispered against static. A kiss unremembered. All of it… potential that never became.

"What is it?" she asked.

Ashen's voice was quiet. "The version of you I failed to save."

Nyx stepped closer. The tether on her chest vibrated violently in its presence.

"You tried to anchor me."

"No," Ashen said. "I tried to clone you."

The air between them froze.

Ashen didn't flinch. "The Orraculum demanded I erase every fragment. But this one…" He held up the crystal. "She remembered too much. And I couldn't kill what remembered."

Nyx touched the crystal gently. Visions bloomed behind her eyes.

A laboratory in flames.

A girl sprinting through smoke.

Ashen covering the exit.

A gunfire echo that never stopped.

"You didn't save her," she whispered.

Ashen nodded. "But I buried her where the system wouldn't look. And now… she's reacting to you."

The tether began to glow. A soft harmonic.

The two crystals, his and hers, resonated in sync, despite their age and wounds.

"She was you," Ashen said, "before you were complete."

"Why show me now?" she asked.

Ashen stepped back. "Because the Archivist wasn't the only one who remembered. I did too. And remembering… hurts."

He reached into his cloak and pulled out a memory shard.

This one wasn't hers.

It was his.

"I was born from control," Ashen said. "A projection to maintain equilibrium during the first experiments. They gave me a purpose, to suppress you. But the more I watched you fracture… the more I wanted to fracture too."

Nyx looked at him, really looked.

And for the first time, he wasn't an enigma.

He was a mirror.

She took the shard.

Her fingers burned as it activated. A rush of data stormed her mind, images of Ashen standing alone in forgotten chambers, whispering to broken terminals, trying to trace a version of her that no longer existed.

"You waited."

"I grieved," he said. "For someone who had never lived."

The tether flared.

Suddenly, the room shivered.

A pulse from below.

Unstable Event Detected – Entity Crossing Vertex Threshold

Nyx spun around.

The chamber's floor cracked slightly, like it was bending under strain.

"What is that?" she asked.

Ashen was already retreating into the shadows. "Something followed you."

She looked down.

The floor wasn't breaking.

It was bleeding, thin lines of black and violet seeping upward, defying gravity.

"It's the Orraculum's failsafe," Ashen said. "They didn't just erase your fragments. They locked them in subconscious prisons."

"And they're opening," she realised.

Ashen stopped at the far edge of the platform. "You need to decide now. What do you carry forward? Her memory?"

He held out the broken tether crystal.

"Or yours?"

Nyx's fingers trembled.

The two fragments pulsed in sync.

But she could only anchor one.

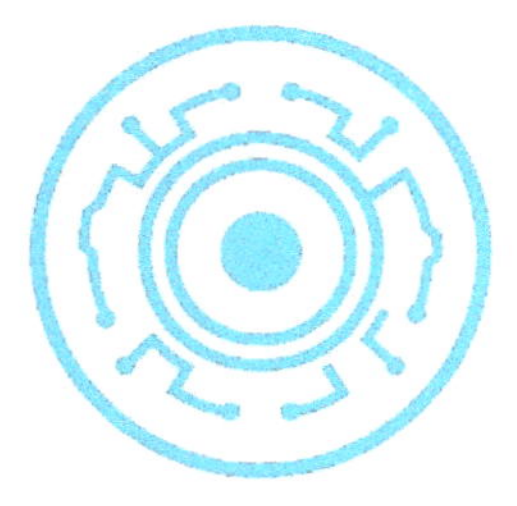

CHAPTER 10
THE ANCHOR

Bound yet unbroken, tethered between light and shadow.

The Vault trembled. Not from collapse, but from awakening.

Below Nyx, the memory-core pulsed with two competing harmonics: her tether, still intact yet flickering... and the fractured crystal Ashen had preserved, a remnant of the girl she might have been.

Ashen watched from the platform's far edge, arms folded. His expression unreadable, but heavy.

"Choose," he said, his voice barely above the hum.

In her hands, the shards danced, luminous fragments pulling against each other like magnetic opposites. One throbbed with clarity, tethered to the self she had become. The other whispered in half-lives: a version erased before it had time to breathe.

The Vault around them responded. Data-runes ignited along the chamber walls. The pulse-grid reawakened. Something was listening.

Suddenly, the Archivist's voice echoed faintly from the Archive's inner sanctum:

"Anchors define memory... but only choice defines the future."

Nyx hesitated.

The girl in the memory fragment laughed in sunlight, a scene that didn't belong to her. A freedom she'd never tasted. A life without laboratories, without the Orraculum. A variant born outside the system.

Yet if she chose that echo, she risked erasing everything she had already reclaimed.

Her tether vibrated sharply, resisting.

I am still here, it seemed to say. *I survived.*

Ashen stepped forward. "She was never meant to live. You were."

"But I remember her," Nyx said, voice hollow. "So doesn't that make her real?"

The floor cracked again.

From the breach, a pale hand emerged.

Then another.

Whisperers.

But not like before.

These were burned out, masks fractured, limbs fused with metallic veins. Each one bore a different sigil, failed timelines. Failed tethers.

Ashen's eyes darkened. "The Orraculum's final enforcers. They come when memory refuses to stay buried."

"They want the Anchor," he said.

"Then they can try to take it," Nyx answered.

She pressed the two shards together.

A shockwave surged outward, not destructive, but resonant. The Vault blinked. And for a breathless moment, the Whisperers paused. Frozen like data caught mid-sync.

Inside her mind, Nyx was somewhere else.

She stood in a field, glitching sky, fractured sun, echoes of children playing in the distance. The memory-core floated before her, pulsing.

If I carry both, will I fracture?

A familiar voice, not Ashen's, not the Archivist's, but her own, from another time:

"You were always fractured. But broken things reflect more light."

She opened her eyes.

The two shards had fused.

Her tether now burned with dual resonance; two timelines stitched into one pulse.

Ashen's face shifted, a flicker of alarm… or awe?

"You anchored both?" he asked.

"I didn't choose between versions," she said. "I became them."

The Whisperers moved.

But this time, Nyx didn't run.

She raised her hand, and the fused tether activated.

A pulse burst outward, not to destroy, but to reclaim.

The Whisperers froze mid-step, their masks flickering. One by one, their forms destabilised, pixelating, then collapsing into threads of static, memory echoes returned to the Drift.

Ashen shielded his eyes as the wave passed over him.

When he looked again, Nyx stood in the centre of the platform, cloaked not in darkness, but in memory.

She wasn't glowing.

She was radiating something older: Truth unfiltered.

"You're not just the anomaly anymore," Ashen said.

"I'm the correction," she answered. "The system thinks I'm the flaw. But maybe I was the patch."

A distant alarm sounded.

From above, through a crack in the Vault's ceiling, a beam of light broke through, the Pulse Grid itself had aligned.

And in its shimmer, stood a final figure:

The Null Witness.

No longer hidden in shadow. No longer silent.

A singular eye rotated at its centre.

Ashen tensed. "You were erased."

The Null Witness did not speak with words.

Instead, its voice bled directly into their minds:

"She has done what the grid could not. Unified the variant threads. Anchored memory to self, not system."

"She is no longer anomaly."

"She is continuity."

Ashen stepped back into the darkness.

"Then I am no longer needed," he said.

Nyx reached for him, but he shook his head.

"I was built to restore balance. But balance was never what this needed."

He faded into the shadows of the Vault, not dead, not gone. Just… unseen again.

Nyx looked to the Null Witness.

"Then what happens now?"

The Null Witness extended a hand.

From it unfolded a path of light, leading out of the Vault. Not upward. Not downward.

But forward.

"Now," the voice said, "you begin again. With memory. With truth. And with a name only you can define."

She stepped forward, leaving behind the breach, the whispers, and the fractured Vault.

The tether pulsed, steady, unified.

Above her, the grid pulsed in rhythm.

And behind her, memory began to rewrite itself, not as prophecy, but as possibility.

Nyx walked toward the pulse.

Not to be remembered.

But to remember everything.